"Can anyone tell me what a contest is?"
Ms. Fair asked.

"It's a race!" said Stephen.

"Sometimes a contest is a race. Very good. What else could a contest be?"

"To see who's the fastest," said Michael.

"That's a race. Think. What else could a contest be?"

"To see who is the best," said Sage.

Ms. Fair nodded. "That's right. Next Friday the school is having an art contest. We're all going to paint pictures to hang in the gym. Prize ribbons will be given to the best painting in each grade."

"How will we know which is the best?" Emily asked.

"Whoever finishes first!" yelled Stephen.

"No," said Ms. Fair. "It won't be a race. There will be a judge."

"A judge puts bad people in jail," said Jake.

"A judge decides things," explained Ms. Fair. "The judge will decide the winners."

"How?" Emily asked.

"The judge will choose which she thinks is the best."

"I think chocolate is the best!" Stephen said.

"Vanilla's better!" said Jake.

"Chocolate!"

"Vanilla!"

"Boys! Quiet! Please remember to raise your hand if you'd like to say something. Yes, Emily?"

"Does the *judge* know which is better?"

"Well, Emily . . . "

"Ms. Fair! Ms. Fair!" Jake waved his hand. "If I lose the art contest will the judge put me in jail?"

"What?! No, of course not. Losing an art contest does not make you a bad person."

"Yeah," said Michael, "just a bad artist."

PETER CATALANOTTO

ALADDIN PAPERBACKS

NEW YORK LONDON TORONTO SYDNEY

On Monday, when Emily painted a butterfly, Ms. Fair said, "Wow! Look at all the amazing colors in those wings."

"Can you show me how to do that?" asked Kelly. "Mine's all muddy."

"Sure!" said Emily.

While Kelly painted a butterfly, Emily painted her family having breakfast.

"Why do you have four mothers?" asked Stephen.

"There's only one mother," Emily explained. "She's just very busy in the morning."

On Tuesday, Emily painted Ms. Fair.
"Why does she have wings?" asked Jonathan.
"Because she's so nice," Emily said. "Like an angel."
Kelly painted a red butterfly.

On Wednesday, Emily painted herself playing with Kelly.
"You both look the same," Sage told Emily.
"That's because she's my best friend. We're just like twins."
Kelly painted a purple butterfly.

EMILY   KELLY

On Thursday, Emily painted her dog.
"How come you made his ears so big?" asked Chris.
"Because Thor hears everything," Emily said.
Kelly painted a green butterfly.

Thursday afternoon, Ms. Fair asked each student to choose
which of their paintings they wanted to enter in the art contest.
Emily chose her painting of Thor. It was her new favorite.

That night, Emily asked her mother which is better: chocolate or vanilla.

"It depends," said her mother. "Some people like chocolate. Some people like vanilla."

"But which one is the best?" asked Emily.

"Whichever one *you* like," her mother replied.

"Oh," said Emily.

"Sleep well, love."

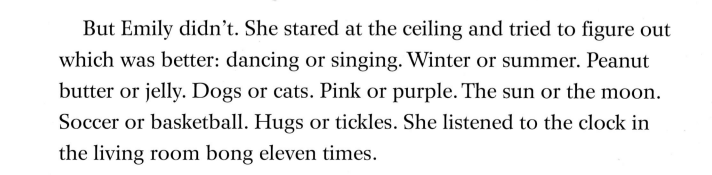

But Emily didn't. She stared at the ceiling and tried to figure out which was better: dancing or singing. Winter or summer. Peanut butter or jelly. Dogs or cats. Pink or purple. The sun or the moon. Soccer or basketball. Hugs or tickles. She listened to the clock in the living room bong eleven times.

Friday morning the entire first grade went to the gym for the art contest. The judge was the principal's mother.

"My cousin is married to an artist," she declared.

Everyone watched the judge inspect each painting. First she looked closely, then she stepped back. She nodded and grunted. Squinted. Rubbed her chin. Crossed her arms and tilted her head. While looking at Kelly's purple butterfly, she noticed Emily's painting.

The judge's face lit up.

"What a gorgeous painting," she exclaimed. "Look at the detail and the amazing colors. A first grader painted this? Incredible! It's absolutely exquisite! What a beautiful rabbit!"

"Ahm . . . pardon me," Ms. Fair said, "but it's a dog."

"A DOG??!!" screeched the judge. "I was attacked by a dog once! Nasty thing ripped my favorite dress! UUUUGHH! I hate dogs!"

Emily's heart twisted.

The judge taped a blue ribbon on Kelly's painting. "I love butterflies," she announced.

Emily took her painting from the wall and carried it to the far end of the playground. She covered it with leaves and sticks. "I'll never paint again," she whispered.

Slowly she returned to the gym. As she joined her class Ms. Fair felt Emily's forehead and said, "You don't look well at all."

When they passed the nurse's
office, Ms. Fair sent Emily in.

The nurse shined a light in Emily's
eyes. Then her ears and nose. She
put a big Popsicle stick in Emily's
mouth and asked her where she hurt.

"I hot."

"You don't feel hot."

Emily gently pushed the stick
out of her mouth and repeated,
"My heart."

The nurse told her to lie on the
couch for a while.

Emily thought, Everyone will be sorry when they find out I'm not going to paint anymore.

Mom will have to think of other things to hang on the refrigerator.

Daddy will have to boast about other things to his boss.

Nana will have to look for other things in the mail.
Joshua will have to watch me do other things after school.

Emily thought and thought until she fell asleep. She
dreamed she was at a picnic and a giant hamburger was
mad at her because she liked hot dogs better. When she
woke up, Kelly was lying next to her.

"Why are you here?" Emily asked.

"I was very dizzy," said Kelly. "Everybody wanted me to make a butterfly for them. The whole class was yelling: 'Me next! I'm next!' My desk was shaking and someone kept bumping my arm. Sage got upset because the painting I did for her didn't look like the one in the contest. And then . . ."

Kelly twirled her hair. She touched each tooth with her tongue. "Then Jake asked me to paint a dinosaur."

Emily waited.

"I don't know how to make a dinosaur," Kelly said quietly. She tapped her shoes together ten times.

"Can you show me?"

"Sure," said Emily.

She took a pencil out of her pocket. On a paper towel she showed her best friend how to draw a dinosaur.

"Wow," Kelly whispered. "You're a good artist."

Emily blushed.

"This isn't the art room," said the nurse.
"You two look well enough to go back
to class now. Hey, great dinosaur!"

Emily told Kelly she needed to get something from the playground.

"Welcome back girls! We're having an art *party* to celebrate *all* our wonderful work." Then Ms. Fair whispered to Emily, "I *knew* one of our special pictures was missing. Now Sage and Jake can go to the cafeteria to get ice cream for everyone."

"What flavor do you want?" Jake asked. "Chocolate or vanilla?"

"Strawberry," said Emily.

"Me too," said Kelly.

Special thanks

to Ms. Fair and her class . . .

and to Emily, for her art.

ALADDIN PAPERBACKS An imprint of Simon & Schuster
Children's Publishing Division   1230 Avenue of the Americas,
New York, NY 10020   Copyright © 2001 by Peter Catalanotto
All rights reserved, including the right of reproduction in whole
or in part in any form.   ALADDIN PAPERBACKS and colo-
phon are trademarks of Simon & Schuster, Inc.   Also available
in an Atheneum Books for Young Readers hardcover edition.
Designed by Michael Nelson   The text of this book was set in
Wilke Roman.   The illustrations for this book were rendered in
watercolor, gouache, and acrylic.   Manufactured in China   First
Aladdin Paperbacks edition December 2006.

2 4 6 8 10 9 7 5 3 1

The Library of Congress has cataloged the hardcover edition as
follows: Catalanotto, Peter. Emily's art / by Peter Catalanotto. —1st
ed. p. cm. "A Richard Jackson book." Summary: Emily paints
four pictures and enters one in the first-grade art contest, but
the judge interprets Emily's entry as a rabbit instead of a dog.
ISBN-13: 978-0-689-83831-6 (hc.)   ISBN-10: 0-689-83831-X (hc.)
[1. Artists—Fiction. 2. Contests—Fiction. 3. Winning and losing—
Fiction.]   I.Title.   PZ7.C26878 Em 2001 [E]—dc21 00029293
ISBN-13: 978-1-4169-2688-7 (pbk.)   ISBN-10: 1-4169-2688-7 (pbk.)

For all children who paint with their hearts
—P. C.